For the immigrants of the world, including Lunita and Teresita
who will never emigrate from my heart. — JA

In memory of Dr. René Sandino Argüello. — LG

The author wishes to thank the Nicaraguan poet and photographer Wálter Gómez.

Text copyright © 2007 by Jorge Argueta
Illustrations copyright © 2007 by Luis Garay

Groundwood Books / House of Anansi Press
110 Spadina Avenue, Suite 801, Toronto, Ontario M5V 2K4
Distributed in the USA by Publishers Group West
1700 Fourth Street, Berkeley, CA 94710

We acknowledge for their financial support of our publishing program the Canada Council for
the Arts, the Government of Canada through the Book Publishing Industry Development
Program (BPIDP) and the Ontario Arts Council.

ONTARIO ARTS COUNCIL
CONSEIL DES ARTS DE L'ONTARIO

Library and Archives Canada Cataloguing in Publication
Argueta, Jorge
Alfredito flies home / by Jorge Argueta ; pictures by Luis
Garay ; translated by Elisa Amado.
Translation of: Alfredito regresa volando a su casa.
ISBN-13: 978-0-88899-585-8
ISBN-10: 0-88899-585-7
1. El Salvador – Juvenile fiction. I. Garay, Luis
II. Amado, Elisa III. Title.
PZ7.A73Al 2007   j861'.64   C2007-900208-0

The illustrations are in acrylic on canvas.
Design by Michael Solomon
Printed and bound in China

Alfredito
Flies Home

Jorge Argueta

PICTURES BY

Luis Garay

TRANSLATED BY

Elisa Amado

GROUNDWOOD BOOKS
HOUSE OF ANANSI PRESS
TORONTO   BERKELEY

My name is Alfredo, just like my father, but everyone calls me Alfredito. I am as happy as a bird today because I'm going back home. Finally, after four whole years in San Francisco, my mother, Adela, my father, my grandmother Serve and I are going to climb on a plane tomorrow and fly back to El Salvador.

"This is a three-week holiday, no more," says my father.

"Yes," agrees my mother. "And during those three weeks we are going everywhere with Ana Gladis — to the beach, to Planes de Renderos, up San Jacinto hill on the teleférico, to Los Chorros and to Sonsonate."

My parents say all this because they think I'll want to stay in El Salvador forever. Because, as they remind me, I never wanted to come here. I cried all the time and even got sick, I felt so bad about leaving home. I was always sad. But this time it will be different. We don't have to go with any Señor Coyote, or run through the mountains, or hide in the trunks of cars the way we did when we first came.

We are all a bit nervous because none of us has ever been on a plane. We haven't stopped talking about the trip since my papi first bought the tickets. When we go to the Mission District to do our week's shopping, we stop in the Chinese stores to buy stuff to give away or sell in El Salvador.

We are taking presents for my sister, Ana Gladis, who stayed behind because she wanted to finish school. Poor thing, she was the only member of our family who didn't come. But she wasn't left all alone because other relatives were there and took care of her. They love her a lot. We also have presents for my tía Toya, my tía Menche and my cousins. And we've got gifts for my friends. I wonder how Chepe, Roxana, Fabio, Chila and my teacher Valentina all are? And how about my parakeets and my dog, Roco?

I'm so excited about seeing them that I sometimes feel like I've got little worms crawling all over me, especially in my stomach. My mami says it's nerves. I say it's happiness.

We have a green duffel bag almost as big as my father. It's full of shoes, dresses, pants, skirts, blouses, undershirts, socks, necklaces of all colors, toys of every kind and cheap perfumes that my mother sells.

Poor green bag. We stuff it full then unpack it almost every night. We weigh it on a scale with other bags that we are filling up. My papi says we can't take more than seventy pounds on the plane.

In Hunter's Point, where we live, I can see planes in the sky from my backyard. I watch them fly by and pray in my head. I'm sure my mami and papi pray, too, though they don't tell me. I think we are all a little scared because planes fly over the clouds.

Finally, the day has come. My mami checks our tickets and says to my papi, "Alfredo, make sure that the tickets and the passports are in order."

"Yes, Adela," he answers, and even though he's done it every day for the past three weeks, he takes out the passports and looks at every page. Then he does the same with our plane tickets, and when he's done he puts them all back in a black bag.

I do the same with my red bag. I open it and take out my toys, one by one, then my pants and my shirts. Then I pack them up again. Last night I slept with all my clothes on, even though our plane doesn't leave until midnight tonight.

We are going to Mission Street this morning to finish our shopping. I'm happy because it's Christmas everywhere. I can feel it in the wind, in the little trees with their red and white stars and the little angel ornaments that fly through their branches, in store windows that are all decorated, in the lampposts hung with wreaths, in the people walking though the street with happy smiles. Some people are sad, though, because they can't see their families in faraway countries, or just because they are poor people who have no houses, or who have to beg. I ask God to help them as he helped me and my family.

We have been walking around for a few hours. At the Ecuadorians' stand my mami tries on a hat and my papi a sweater. But in the end we don't buy anything. We only came down to pass the time. It's time to go home, check our bags, our tickets and our passports all over again.

"What time is it, Mami?"

"Time to get dressed," she says. "Your uncle Mincho will be here soon to take us to the airport."

My mami hasn't noticed that I've been ready since yesterday. My papi, standing in the doorway, is watching the cars go by. "Adela, are you ready?" he asks. "My brother will be here soon."

"I'm ready," says Mami. "You go get ready yourself."

My family is a little bit crazy, I think to myself. My mami checks the bathroom and the kitchen to make sure she has turned everything off. She waters the plants again and sweeps the floor. She looks in the mirror and fixes her hair. My papi stands by the phone like he's expecting a call. Then he walks up and down until he's back where he started —waiting for Uncle Mincho's van.

Finally Tío Mincho drives up with my tía Laura and my grandmother Serve.

It's a good thing Tío Mincho's van is so big, because my grandmother's suitcases are as big as ours. We can barely all fit in.

Before we leave, my tío Mincho hands my father three envelopes and says, "Please give these to Toyita, to my father and to Juan Patías. Say hello to them and tell them we love them and miss them and that we hope to see them soon."

My tía Laurita also has envelopes with her parents' names, Jesús and Menche, written on them. "Please do me a big favor and go see my parents and give them these," she says.

I can hear a sadness in their voices. It seems like they are saying, please take my eyes with you so they can see my parents.

The airport is big and full of happy, sad or nervous people. They are dragging big bags and little bags of every color from one place to another. They are going to every part of El Salvador. Girls, boys, old ladies, old men, mothers and fathers, and all kinds of teenagers. The airport is like a huge market but people aren't buying anything. Instead they are walking fast, then crying, then hugging.

While we stand in line to give our bags to the airplane, my tío Mincho comes up to me with a mischievous grin and whispers in my ear, "Don't go talking in English so much with your father, okay?"

I look at him and answer, "Okay, Uncle."

My father, who overhears, laughs and says in his special English, "Dunt wurri, sar."

He is still learning and he meant to say, "Don't worry, sir." But no matter how much Papi tries, his English comes out all broken, like he is biting his tongue. We all laugh because we love each other and hug one last time before handing over the bags and going to the waiting room.

My granny Serve has tears in her eyes. I know she wishes everyone could come with us. She looks over her shoulder at Tío Mincho and Laurita. When I see her pretty old lady face looking so sad, I cry, too, and give her a hug.

Now there is nothing left to do but wait for the plane.

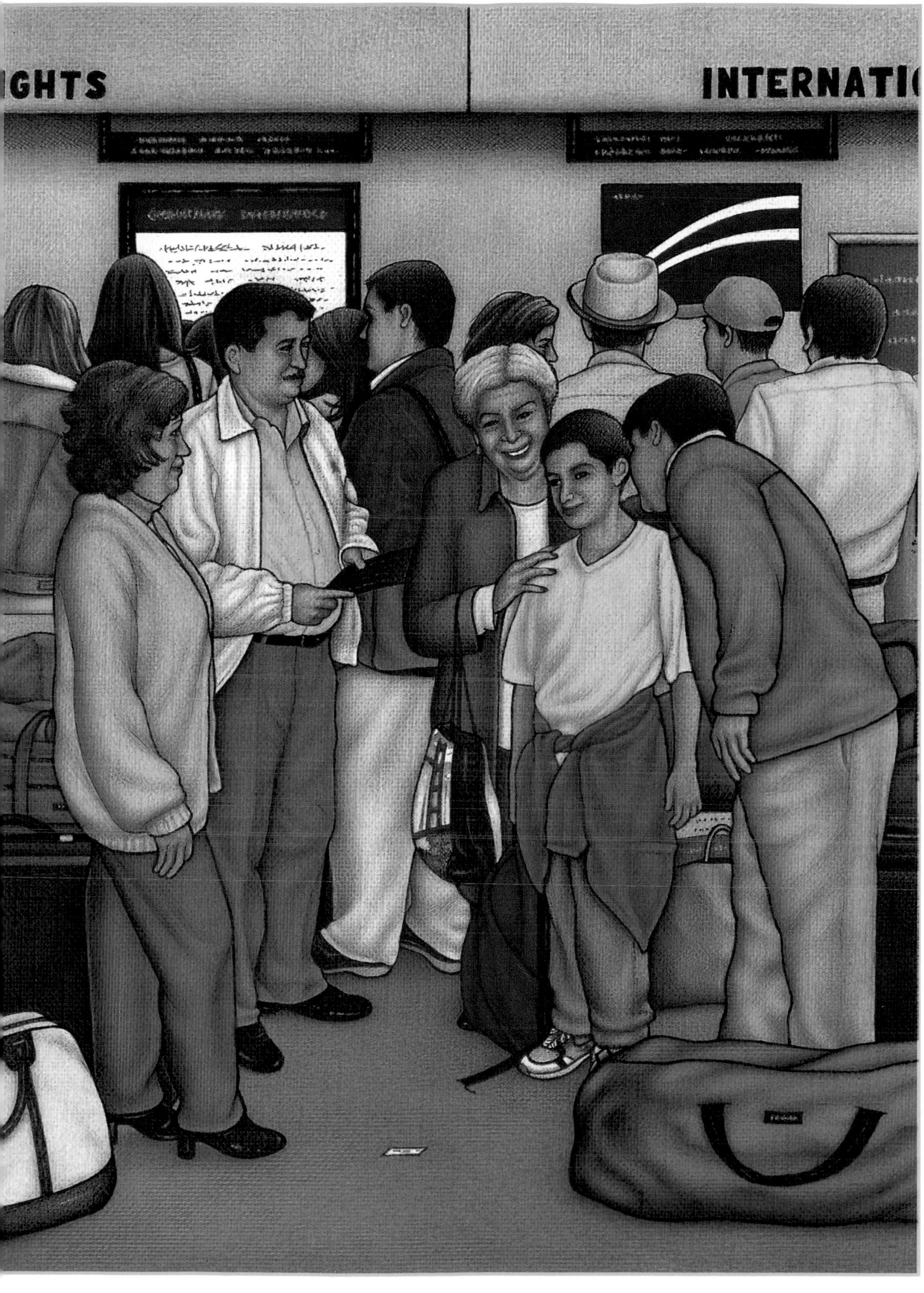
IGHTS
INTERNATI

In this room there are gigantic windows. We can see lots of planes outside. I stand and watch workers dragging little trucks that go back and forth loaded with suitcases.

I feel a little bit scared mixed in with being happy. I think about my friends at school, here in San Francisco, and about the family and friends that I will see in El Salvador.

Finally, it's time to get on the plane. My papi silently takes my sweaty hand and makes me feel safe. We walk through a narrow tunnel like a snake's belly. At the end I can see a young woman of the kind who works on planes. She checks our tickets and invites us, really politely, to get on. I can't believe it. I turn around and look at my father who is just behind me, but he looks astonished, too. I think we all feel the same. Can this be a dream or are we really going home?

———————————— ✳ ————————————

Of course, my seat is by the window. I can see everything. The plane is moving. We tighten our seat belts and look at each other without saying a word. We are amazed by what is happening. The plane starts to go faster. The captain says some words. One of the young women stands in the middle and moves like a ballet dancer, telling us what to do in an emergency. We laugh nervously. I touch the plane to make sure that I'm really traveling on one, and I touch it to see how it feels. I think, isn't it too heavy to go up? The plane starts to move faster. It makes sounds. Everything shakes.

Finally, the plane jumps like a frog and leaves everything behind. There are only little lights down there, like jewels. Some are moving. They are white and red. They must be cars. They look like little ant lights from up here.

"We're flying!" I shout out in a trembly voice.

My mami sits next to me with my papi beside her and Abuela Serve across the aisle. Their faces are all looking my way, not to see me but to try to see through the window.

My eyes are wide open and I can't stop looking out. Even though it's dark, I think I might see God sitting on a star. The plane feels like a whale slowly swimming through the sea of the sky.

I don't know how much time has passed, but I think it must be a few hours because outside everything is suddenly changing color. It's turned blue. There are some very white clouds next to the plane. I think that maybe they have followed us.

Down below, everything looks green and square or sometimes like a city framed by yellow and green lines. Mother Earth like a field of corn.

And suddenly, there it is — our beloved volcano, Quezaltepec. I feel the plane start to go down. My heart speeds up.

"We are arriving in El Salvador," says my grandmother Serve excitedly. My parents smile.

Trees look like green cotton. The plane is flying lower. I have little worms crawling around in my belly again. Bang. We are back on the ground.

Over the loudspeaker I hear the pilot say, "Welcome to El Salvador." Some passengers clap happily.

The door opens and a wave of hot wind fills the plane. El Salvador's heat is rushing in to greet us.

When we go out, there is a crowd just past the place where people pick up their bags. They have come to meet the plane. The people inside and the people outside are screaming. They are happy and nervous. They are jumping up in the air, hoping to see their relatives. The airport fills with hugs, shrieks and happiness. People kiss and look each other over from top to bottom. It's like a carnival.

My mami starts to cry. "There's my daughter, Ana, Ana, Ana Gladis!"

Then we all scream until she sees us and runs over to hug us. Behind her comes my tía Toya, drying her tears. After her comes my tía Menche, with some boys and girls I don't know. Then I realize that they are my cousins. Miguelito has grown so big, and so have María José, Bryant, Kevin, Alejandro and Gabriela. There are so many of them and they look so different. And there are other cousins who have been born. For a while I can't tell who is who. At first I feel a bit strange, but in the truck going to the house we start to talk and play and everything changes. Then it's as though we have never been apart.

My heart feels like Christmas exploding in my chest.

Everyone talks at once. They are so happy. "Let's go to Comalapa," says my papi. "I want to eat some real pupusas."

"Yes, yes, yes," everyone yells back.

When we get there I see women balancing baskets on their heads, swaying as they sell mangos, zapotes, jocotes, nances, nísperos, cocos, pupusas, tamales pizques, corn tamales, chicken tamales and pork tamales. Everything looks delicious. Even the buses are like candies with their bright paint and decorations.

When we get home my grandpa Miguel is waiting for me. His smile doesn't fit on his face. And there are more girl cousins and more boy cousins, more aunts and more uncles, and now some friends. Everyone is so happy. Everyone has come to see us.

I can hardly believe that I am back in my little house. Here are the brick walls, the tables, the chairs, the black and red floor in part of the house and the earth floor in the other. The lamina roof and the tile roof. The stones around the outside, San Jacinto hill behind, in front of the volcano, Quezaltepec. The mango trees, the orchard. They all seem to say welcome. I stop and look at the hibiscus bush. Parakeets are flying and dancing through its branches, squawking their crazy songs. They are welcoming me, too.

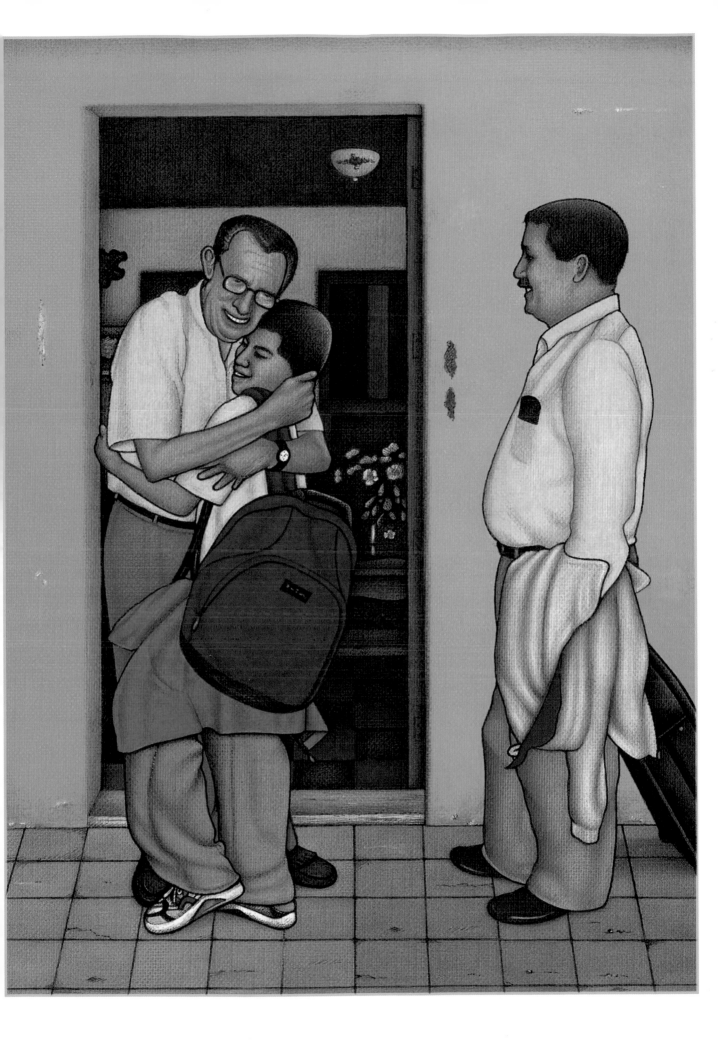

My friend Roxana walks in with a puppy. "Alfredito, do you know who this is?"

"No," I answer.

"It's one of Roco's babies. His wife Negra had four puppies."

My grandma Serve says, "Now you are a grandpa, too."

Everyone laughs while Roxana, my cousins and I run off to look for Roco, his wife and his babies. "Roco! Roco! Roco!" I shout.

Suddenly Roco appears, wagging his little tail, saying, where have you been? He jumps into my arms.

"Roco, Roco, how are you?"

Roco licks my face and talks to me in his doggy voice. "I hear you are a dad," I say, crying. When I put him down, Roco jumps, barks and whirls around. He wants me to follow him. Around the corner, they have fixed him a little house. There are his puppies. I pick them all up and we play with them for a long time.

My father's friends have come to take him to play football, his favorite sport. "Tío Tigre, here's a ball. Let's go over to the soccer field."

"Uncle Tiger" has been his nickname since he was a boy. They call him that because he was always the fastest at climbing up to cut mangos from the tree.

This is the best Christmas of my life. I love listening to Christmas carols on the radio and firecrackers exploding in the air. There are whistlers that shoot up, mortars that explode loudly and trail colored streamers, buscaniguas that follow you around on the floor, as well as crazy machine guns and little volcanoes that shoot out stars.

Now it's midnight. The sound of fireworks is deafening as we all shout, "Happy Christmas!"

I don't know how many days have gone by. I don't ever feel tired or hot, though my mami does. I just want to play and listen to people talking — and they talk without stopping, night after night! I think their mouths must hurt. They talk and talk and talk. I don't think they've stopped since we got here. They laugh and cry and sing and tell stories.

Our bags have all been given away. One is for Rosa. I don't even know who got the others. Everyone got something and they all loved their presents. My friend Chepe wears the Golden Gate T-shirt I brought him every day.

Today we have come to see my abuelita Paz and my abuelo Jando. They live in the cemetery. We brought them lots of flowers. First we go to see my grandmother. My mother talks to her as if she could hear. "Listen, Mamá, forgive me for not having been here when you went."

"Yes, Pacita," says my father. "It all happened so fast we couldn't make it. Can you see how big your grandson has grown?"

I don't say anything. I wait for her to answer, but she doesn't. She's under the ground. Then we walk a little way until we get to where my grandpa Jando lives now. My mother and father talk to him without saying words, and then we give him flowers and say good-bye.

When we leave the cemetery, the sun shines on our backs.

I say, "I'm glad the cemetery is so full of little birds and is nice and hot so my grandparents don't feel cold and alone."

The days are going so fast, it seems like they are being blown away by the wind. We've had so much fun, I'd like to hold onto them. But I can't.

I don't want to go. I want to go on playing mica, hide-and-seek, flying kites and climbing trees with my friends and my cousins.

"Mami, I feel free here. I don't want to leave El Salvador," I say.

She looks at me but she doesn't answer.

Because we only have two more days before we leave, tomorrow we are going to have a piñata to say good-bye.

We already bought one, a huge red and green mango. "Chapudito," says my father. We've filled it with candy, confetti, surprises and coins. The house is full of colored balloons and we've hung up so many colored paper streamers, the place looks like a rainbow. On a table there's a huge chocolate cake that looks delicious. Next to it are huge jugs of juice — one of tamarind and the other horchata.

Finally, it's time to break the piñata. My father is in charge of swinging it up and around. My mami covers our eyes with a handkerchief so we can't see it. We hit out wildly with an old broom handle. The mango dances up and down and when the candies begin to fall out, we all scream and dive onto the floor to grab the treats.

We are so happy, even Roco, his wife Negra and his puppies look like they are dancing.

No one wants the party to end. I don't want tomorrow to come. When I think about the plane I feel like crying. I look around and sigh deeply.

My tía Toya who is very wise comes up to me and says, "Don't be sad, mi'jo. God willing, next year you'll be back and we'll all be together again."

Next year, I think. It's so far away. And I sigh again.

In the truck on the way to the airport, everyone is crying. We cheer each other up by taking photos.

"Give Mincho, Laura, everyone our love," say Tía Toya and Tía Menche, drying their eyes.

My sister, Ana, doesn't say anything, but she looks at us as though she wants her looking to tell us how much she loves us, and that she wishes she could engrave us on her heart.

We say good-bye and get back on the plane. This time we sleep the whole trip.

When we get to the house I open the door and notice that the light on the message machine is blinking. There are messages and some of them must be for me.

I suddenly feel a bit happy. I just realized, I'm lucky. I have two homes after all.

Glossary

Abuela / abuelita — grandmother.

Abuelo / abuelito — grandfather.

Buscaniguas — firecrackers that stay on the ground.

Chapudito — red, rosy.

Cocos — coconuts.

Comalapa — a place to buy food on the roadside near the town of Comalapa.

Horchata — a drink made from rice.

Jocotes — tropical fruit.

Lamina — Corrugated tin.

Los Chorros — a place where cascades of falling water have created natural pools.

Mica — tag.

Mi'jo — my son.

Nances — tiny, round, sweet fruit.

Nísperos — loquat fruit.

Planes de Renderos — a national park.

Pupusas — corn tortillas with a filling.

San Jacinto hill — a well-known hill in San Salvador.

Sonsonate — a department (like a province or state) in western El Salvador.

Tamales pizques — tamales made with corn dough and filled with beans.

Teleférico — funicular.

Zapotes — fleshy, sweet fruit.